JAYDEN THOMPSON

STARS IN THE SKY

A DIAMOND IN THE ROUGH NOVELLA

Second edition
ISBN: 979-8-9924339-1-3

*To my parents, since Dad was upset I didn't
dedicate the last book to him.*

(He was joking. Sort of.)

STARS IN THE SKY

ONE

He wasn't coming back.

The rough bark of the tree dug into my back through my tank top. I fiddled with the cowboy hat in my lap, bending the brim this way and that, staring at the trees in front of me without really seeing them. It had been a full twenty-four hours since Ethan took off through those trees, his long strides eating up the distance, leaving me to listen to his footsteps fade away until nothing but silence remained.

He hadn't even glanced back at me.

The memory had a fresh round of tears rising to the surface. I was glad there wasn't a mirror out here—my face would be red and blotchy, streaked with tears, my blue hair stuck to my sweat-slicked neck in a very unladylike manner. I was a mess, but few things in this world weren't. This was the wastelands, after all. Everything was ravaged and broken.

I stared at the trees Ethan disappeared into and realized with a horrifying amount of certainty that he was not coming back.

Which was fine. I told him to go. Screamed it at him, actually. I'd survived two years in the wastelands after Avery; I could make it a whole lot more without Ethan.

I forced myself to stand up, my legs aching with the movement. It was time to leave; the Viper's base was just on the other side of the tree line. There was no telling when Nico would return, when he would begin his hunt anew. Really, I should have left yesterday, but I'd hung around in hopes that Ethan would cool off and come back.

"Stupid assassin," I muttered.

A low snarl answered me. My heart jumped into my throat as I turned to see a mutant, its bloodshot eyes fixed on me. Cursing under my breath, I palmed a knife and spread my feet apart, shifting into a fighting stance as it lumbered near.

Three stumbling steps brought it to me. I slashed upwards with the knife, grunting as the blade made contact with its neck. Blood sprayed. The mutant gurgled, a horrifying sound if there ever was one, and collapsed at my feet. I shivered as its hands twitched once before falling still.

It was definitely time to go.

I scooped up my fallen bags, grunting at their weight before remembering that we'd shoved them full of the extra ammunition Ethan had nicked from the Viper's base. It was tempting to just leave it all behind—the knife I killed the mutant with was the blue-hilted one he'd chosen specifically for me—but I wasn't stupid. Supplies were supplies. It didn't matter where it came from or who gathered it. I reached into the pocket of my backpack to confirm my sketchbook was there, only to remember at the last second it was stowed away in Ethan's pack.

"Damn it!" I hissed. It wasn't a big deal—I could always find another book. Ethan was no doubt burning the purple sketchbook along with anything else of mine he had. The thought should not have bothered me as much as it did.

Another growl came from the treeline. I backed away, eyes skipping over the campsite to make sure I hadn't left anything else behind. Then I turned on my heel and sprinted away.

The journey back to my church was largely uneventful. A few stray mutants wandered across my path, and I put them down without mercy. I almost found myself wishing for some trouble, for something to happen so I could have a distraction.

Hours dragged by. The night was spent under the shelter of a large oak tree, but I was gone again by morning. Eventually the landscape turned familiar and I found myself walking up the hill to the church. The sight eased something in my chest. It wasn't perfect—birds had made nests in the bell tower, my homemade stained glass windows didn't look as good as the real deal, and it was a far cry from a secure fortress—but it felt like home. It was enough to bring the hint of a smile to my face, a gesture that had been lacking for longer than I liked to admit.

Everything will be fine, I told myself. The world had righted itself after Avery and it would damn well do so again.

I unlocked the back door, letting out a sigh of relief as I entered the building. It was a refuge—that's what it had been long before the Virus ever hit, before there were mutants roaming the land. Churches had been houses of worship, sanctuaries against the evil of the world. At its base, it was just a building, but what it stood for was much more important.

I still believed that, even if nobody else did.

All of my belongings were still in place. The shelves full of trinkets twinkled in the sunlight coming from the colored windows. I tossed my bags aside and ambled down the aisle, my thumbs hooked in the pockets of my denim shorts and the cowboy hat sitting at an angle on my head. These trinkets had been collected over weeks and months. I told Ethan they were a monument to the beauty civilization used to have. My intention was to have this building full of such beauty that if something ever happened to me, someone could walk into this room in a few days or a few years and realize there was more beauty in the world than most people led you to believe. There were vases full of blooming flowers. Paintings on canvases. Windchimes and musical instruments. Little glass figurines. Pictures of happy couples and smiling children.

There was *beauty,* even in a broken world.

My eyes fell on a broken snowglobe, shoved on a shelf in the corner. The water inside was long gone, the glass nothing but a few jagged shards still clinging to one side.

The same snowglobe Ethan had broken the first time he came in here.

You're like a bull in a china shop.

My breathing turned ragged.

I wished I could get over it. Ethan probably had—he was no doubt halfway across the state by now, ambling along without even a second thought, perfectly content now that I wasn't making him *weak*.

His entire argument was stupid. If he wasn't so damn tall, I would have slapped him across the face until he saw reason.

"It's stupid," I said aloud. I glared at the snowglobe. "*You're* stupid!"

I picked it up and hurled it across the room. It thunked against the far wall, the last of the glass falling out. Heat rose inside of me, and I ripped off the hat, trying to find air. I wanted more things to throw, things I could break, something I could rip apart with my bare hands, but I'd worked too hard on everything in the church to destroy it all in a fit of rage.

So I marched outside, picked up the biggest rock I could find, and hurled it through the window of the first house on the street.

The merry twinkling of glass was very calming.

I scooped up another rock and sent it flying through a window on the second floor. My hand was poised to do it again when my gaze snagged on something two houses down. Twenty-something mutant corpses were piled on top of each other in front of a porch on the verge of collapse—the very same porch I'd clambered on top of to get away from the herd when it appeared unexpectedly at the end of the street, blocking me from getting back to the church. Ethan had appeared like a knight in shining armor, if knights wore t-shirts and cowboy boots and packed around AR-15s to kill zombies with.

This entire town had him written all over it. I hadn't even known him that long and he was everywhere. There was the spot where we stood when I spoke to him the first time. As I stormed back to the church, I saw the tree he leaned against while I teased him before the two Vipers had shown up to try and kill us. Back inside was the corner of the church where he slept, the stage where we played Dare, the spot behind the pulpit where we kissed.

I felt like screaming. Ethan had been the one who wanted to leave—it wasn't fair that *I* was the one haunted by him. At least with Avery, escaping to the wastelands meant escaping everything associated with him. The only reminder I had was the scar on my abdomen.

No—I had to stop comparing them. Ethan was nothing like Avery. *Nothing* like him.

A tear dripped down my cheek. I angrily wiped it away as I stormed to the back room, hunting through my supplies until I found a fresh book to draw in. This one was simpler with a plain black cover and thick pages. I yanked my markers out of my pack and plopped down behind the pulpit with every intention to draw my frustrations out on the page.

But my vision went blurry. A wet spot formed on the page of the book, followed by another, and then I was crying in earnest, throwing the book away and hugging my knees to my chest.

It wasn't fair.

It wasn't fair.

It wasn't fair.

And yet I still missed him.

I buried my head between my knees, curling up in a tight ball with my back pressed against the pulpit. My fingers curled around my necklace. The jagged half of the broken heart dug into my thumb as I gripped it tight enough to draw blood.

My sister Lucy had found the matching necklaces while on a supply run in what once was a mall. I'd been sixteen at the time, and Lucy—two years my elder—had just started her assigned work in the Houston Safe Zone. I had waited by the gates after school for her to arrive, growing more worried by the minute. Then she'd shown up with the rest of her group, smiling broadly and bearing a present. After Avery stabbed me, Lucy had been the one to tell me to run away, but she'd made me promise to never take off the necklace. *We'll both keep our necklaces on,* she'd said, fitting the two halves of the heart together, *and every night we can go and look at the same stars and know the other is okay. You are going to be okay, Laiken. I know it.*

I hadn't even touched the clasp of the necklace since. And every night, I'd peer up at the stars in the sky, even if it was just for a moment, because it reminded me of all the nights Lucy and I would sit outside and watch constellations glitter in the night as kids. My sister had been the one person who was never annoyed with me, the one who always returned my smile even when I knew she didn't feel like it.

I wished she was here. What I wouldn't give to be able to hug her right now.

Lucy probably thought I was dead.

Another sob racked my body. In the last two years I learned to be okay with being alone. But that didn't stop times like this when I wanted nothing more than to have someone by my side.

We all need a friend.

I thought Ethan was here to stay. That I would have someone for a long time.

But then he left. Called me a risk he couldn't afford and just walked away.

I cried even harder and tried not to think of what a mess I was being right now. But a noise from behind had me freezing, struggling to control my breathing as silent tears flowed down my cheeks. There was a creak of wood, a rush of wind, and what sounded a whole lot like footsteps.

Ethan. He had come back. I was on my feet in an instant, whirling around with a sigh of relief. "Lord a'mercy, Bull, I—"

But it wasn't Ethan who stood in the center of the church, a rifle in his hands and a dozen people standing behind him.

Nico De La Cruz gave me a slow, cruel smile. "Hello, sweetheart."

TWO

My heart leapt into my throat. I stumbled back, slamming into the glass wall that partitioned off the baptistry. Nico surged forward, but I drew my pistol and pointed it at him with shaking hands. I found myself grateful for the mandatory training back in the Safe Zones that required each able-bodied citizen to learn how to use a weapon, because this gun was the only thing standing between me and the Vipers.

And I knew exactly how to use it.

He stopped short. "Put the gun down."

"Get out of my church," I snapped.

The other Vipers pressed forward. They didn't explain why they were here, how they had found the church, and I certainly didn't ask. They had no good reason for being here, that was for sure. I recognized Ren and Josh alongside the leader of the gang from the day Ethan and I had snuck into their base. The rest were unfamiliar to me. One nod from Nico had Josh and two others circling around to my side.

"Get out!" I screamed, waving the gun between them and Nico.

He kept smiling, his dark eyes glinting as he mounted the first step. "Why don't you tell us where the giant is?"

"He's in the back," I said. "And he will kill every one of you."

It didn't come out with quite the bite I had intended. Nico smirked. "Liar," he purred. "There was only one set of tracks coming this way."

My racing thoughts screeched to a halt. Nico must have tracked me—that's why the Vipers were here, how they found my church. *Dammit.*

I tried to inch away as he got closer, but I was backed against the wall with a dozen guns pointed at my face. There was nowhere to go. Panic set in as Nico and Josh approached from opposite sides, forcing me to choose one to aim the gun at. I settled on Nico.

He shook his head at me. "Come on, sweetheart. Either pull the trigger or put the gun down. Don't play these games with me."

My finger tightened on the trigger. There was no way I'd be able to kill them all. I was no assassin. But from this angle, I could put a bullet through Nico's skull and at least kill him before the others took me down.

But I'd only used a gun to take down mutants before. Never a living person.

If Ethan were here, he would have already slaughtered them all. But I lowered the gun to the ground and kicked it to Nico's feet.

His smile grew. "Good choice."

"Get out," I whispered, but my leverage was gone. Josh handed off his gun and grabbed me by the arm. I pulled against him, but his grip might as well have been made out of stone. He wrenched my arms behind my back as another Viper produced a length of rope.

"Why are you doing this?" I demanded. I hissed as the rope bit into my wrists. "This is madness!"

Nico barked a laugh. "This is the wastelands. What's the saying? *We're all mad here.*"

"That's from *Alice in Wonderland,* you uneducated idiot!"

He blinked, confused, and I realized that not everyone had access to the classic book section in the Houston public library like I had. I hissed at him, trying to get away, but my wrists were firmly tied behind my back. Nico smirked at me before turning to his assembled crowd.

"Troy," he barked. The leader from the other day perked up. "Check the back rooms and make sure nobody's back there. I don't want any surprises. The rest of you, find their supplies."

They scattered. Nico shoved me to the ground, and I watched the Vipers sift through my stuff. Troy realized almost instantly that the majority of my supplies were stashed in the back. The Vipers carried it outside one box at a time, grinning at each other as they studied their spoils. Food and clothes and weapons and ammo—they took it all. Nico watched them from where he stood beside me.

"I must say, this has definitely been worth it." He sneered down at me. "And to think, this all started with a little old backpack. If you had just handed it over, we wouldn't be doing this."

I glared at him. "It wasn't yours to take. Neither is any of this."

He clicked his tongue. "That's a shame, isn't it?"

Josh gave me a bright smile from where he stood next to his boss.

Troy appeared on Nico's other side. "The back rooms have been cleared out, boss. We've got everything worth taking. And there's no sign of the giant anywhere."

Troy seemed to have healed up nicely since our last en-counter. There was no sign of the bullet wound Ethan gave him. But he still remembered it, apparently, because he refused to make direct eye contact with me.

"Good," Nico said. He jerked his chin at the shelves in front of us. "Destroy all this."

"No!"

The word burst out of me before I could stop it. Nico arched a dark brow. "Oh, you wanted to keep all this? I'm sorry." He glanced at Troy. "Hurry up with it."

He grinned and gave Nico a salute before gesturing to the other Vipers. One hefted a metal baseball bat over his shoul-der, and I cried out as he smashed through a row of glass figurines. Another Viper sent a vase crashing to the ground.

"Stop!" I screamed.

"Shut up," Josh snapped. "It's all junk anyway."

It wasn't *junk*. Not to me. I watched Troy pull out a knife and slash through paintings, a Viper behind him taking pictures out of their frames and ripping them in two, letting the pieces flutter to the ground. One kicked over an entire shelf, creating a domino effect with every other shelf on that side of the room. Glass was shattered, tables overturned, flowers crushed underfoot. The wooden pulpit was smashed to pieces only a couple feet away.

But what broke me was when Nico picked up a ceramic angel, weighing it in his hand.

And then sent it hurtling through the nearest window.

The rest of the Vipers set their sights on the stained glass windows, laughing and cajoling each other as they threw things at them, shattering months of work in a matter of seconds. The guy with the baseball bat made sure to knock every shard down, leaving gaping holes where colorful glass murals once stood. I didn't even have the strength to cry any more as I watched them destroy the church. Josh's hand on my shoulder was the only thing holding me upright.

Troy ambled up to us, hands in his pockets and a shit-eating grin on his face. "I think that does it."

Nico angled his head. "One more thing."

He dug a can of spray paint from his bag. My throat constricted as he walked up to the baptistry, shaking the can with a smile. The other Vipers shared grins.

Nico held up the can to the mural on the baptistry and began writing.

THE VIPERS WERE HERE.

The letters were bold and blood red, paint dripping down the mural of the lake and mountains. I felt like falling apart all over again; that mural had been the prettiest thing about this church, and Nico had ruined it.

"Now it's done." He tossed the can away and hauled me to my feet. "Let's go. I want to get home before the giant catches wind of what we've done."

"He's gone," I said, my voice distant to my own ears. "He's not coming back."

"I doubt that, sweetheart. Let's move."

Josh and Ren took over, one holding each arm as they escorted me through the front doors. I didn't have the heart to look back at the shattered remains of the church, of my home for two years. I'd poured my heart and soul into that building, and all it took was ten minutes to see it stripped bare.

The Vipers made quick work of dividing the goods from the back room between them. On top of the dozen that came inside the church, there were at least that many more waiting outside. Nico had brought his entire army along, it seemed, perhaps expecting Ethan to show up.

Which was actually very smart of him, though it didn't help me any.

We didn't stay at the church for long. As soon as everything was packed away and ready to go, Nico took off walking, motioning for a man bearing a map to take the lead. Ren and Josh remained on either side of me, keeping me in place. They shouldn't have worried so much; I'd only gotten back this morning, and the hours I'd spent crying since had zapped what little remained of my energy. I wouldn't have ran away if they untied me and begged me to go for it.

We walked until nightfall. I didn't say a word the entire time, not quite listening to Josh and Troy arguing over the best way to tie a knot. The Vipers were a tight bunch, it seemed, and they were effective, too. They had camp set up within a matter of minutes. Nico directed everything from atop a tree stump, shouting orders down like a king to his minions.

"Great," he said once everything was done. "Now tie her to a tree and get the night watch sorted out."

Her being me. I didn't fight as I was pulled to a nearby oak tree. Josh untied me and let me stay that way long enough to eat and to relieve myself behind a bush, but Nico was quick to have me tied back up. I slumped against the tree and stared blankly at the bonfire the Vipers had constructed in the middle of their camp.

"It's okay," a soft voice murmured. "We're not going to hurt you."

I glanced up to see Ren, his blonde hair gilded with gold in the firelight.

"I don't believe that," I said.

"The boss just wants to get to your friend. He's the one we're really after." He shook his head. "We're not going to hurt *you.*"

I ripped my gaze away. "You might believe that, but I'm sure Nico has other plans. Besides, you hurt me plenty by what you did to my church."

He bit his lip. "I'm sorry."

I looked at him again, really looked, taking in the expression on his face. He looked almost… *ashamed?*

Ren, I remembered, had been the one the most scared to fight Ethan. To continue searching for us.

Maybe I could use that to my advantage.

"Nobody said *you* had to do this," I said softly. "If you don't want this to happen, then stop it. Ethan and I didn't do anything to start this. It was *Nico* who instigated and continued this fight. You know that." I looked at him with pleading eyes. "You have the power to stop this, Ren. And you *should*, because it's the right thing to do."

Ren looked at me for a few long moments.

"I'm sorry," he said again.

Then he walked away.

THREE

Tied against the tree all night, I slept poorly. The same went for every other night of our journey, my nights spent trying to find comfort even when the bark of the tree dug through my thin tank top and rocks poked my legs and rear end. The days were hot and humid. The trip had been much shorter for just Ethan and I, but the sheer number of Vipers—all weighed down with the goods from the church—dragged it out longer. Thankfully the sun went in by the second day, a sprinkle of rain giving us relief from the Texas heat. By the time we made it to the Viper's base, the air was heavy with the promise of a good thunderstorm.

I barely talked the entire trip. Nico asked me several times if I knew where *the giant* was, but he gave up after I said no for the third time. The rest of the Vipers made a point not to talk to me—or to even look at me, in Ren's case—so I walked along in silence, letting my curtain of blue hair shield my face from view.

The trees thinned up ahead, and several of the Vipers let out cheers as their base came into view. Bile rose in my throat. Josh shoved me forward, herding me to the sprawling building covered in graffiti and weeds. Panic seized my body at the sight of it, at the thought of being trapped in those walls.

"There's no point in this!" I shouted at Nico. He ambled along at the front of the pack, but he paused at my words, allowing me to catch up to him. "Ethan's not coming for me! Just let me go!"

My words were interrupted by a crack of lightning that cleaved the sky in two. Even Nico flinched as the bottom opened up and rain speared for the ground, a roar of thunder almost drowning out his response.

"We wouldn't want to kick you out into this mess, sweetheart," he said with sweet venom, signaling his men to head inside. "We don't throw women out into thunderstorms. It's called chivalry."

I studied him for a few heartbeats.

Then I kicked him between the legs.

Nico doubled over with a howl. Josh tackled me to the ground, pinning me to the dirt with such force I could barely breathe. But I was grinning too hard to care. I wasn't a person to delight in another's pain, but the string of curses Nico let out were extremely heartwarming.

"Lock her up," he snarled.

I was wrenched to my feet. Nico's dark eyes burned with hatred, but I smiled at him as I was pushed past.

Ethan would have been proud.

The thought sent an unpleasant jolt through me. Ethan wasn't here. He was gone. I had to stop thinking about him.

Josh hauled me inside the base before I could get soaked through with rain. His jaw was set, his fingers curled around my bicep hard enough to leave a bruise. Ren was a bit gentler from my other side, but still firm enough to keep me moving even when I struggled against them. I twisted in their grip, nearly dislodging their hands.

Josh pulled the entire operation to a halt by grabbing the front of my shirt and pulling me forward until I wasn't but an inch from his face.

"You are going to behave, sweetheart," he spat. "Stop squirming. Stop trying to get away. You either walk on your own, or I will truss you up and drag you. Understand?"

I debated kicking him like I did Nico, but I didn't think it would help my situation any, however satisfying it might be. I gave a restrained dip of my head in answer. Josh shoved me forward. This time, I didn't protest as they led me through the halls.

I tried to keep track of the halls we went down, what turns we took, but I soon became convinced they were leading me in circles to confuse me. Either way, I ended up inside what looked to be an office of sorts—or had been back in the day. A bulletin board hung crookedly on one wall. Papers were pinned to it, so aged they were unreadable. There was a swivel chair and a file cabinet missing its drawers but no desk. Instead there was a pile of blankets on the floor and a metal bar with a pair of handcuffs dangling from them.

I wasn't the Vipers' first prisoner, it seemed.

Josh whipped out a knife. I flinched, expecting him to slash at me, but he merely cut the bindings around my arms. One handcuff was placed around my wrist, the other end attached to the metal bar. It didn't give me much room to move around, but at least the blankets were in place. It was better than the tree was.

"Troy!" Josh barked.

He appeared in the doorway, his brown hair slick with rain.

"Guard her," he snapped, jerking a thumb in my direction. He and Ren filed out, leaving me alone with Troy. He plopped down in the swivel chair, using one foot to kick it around in a circle like I saw kids do back in school.

"You're immature," I muttered under my breath.

He grabbed the edge of the file cabinet to stop himself. "What did you just say?"

I gave him an innocent look. "Nothing."

His eyes narrowed. I made a show of lying down on the blankets—which were actually quite comfortable compared to sleeping on the ground. Troy relaxed and went back to spinning the chair around.

Days of travel and the weight of grief had taken their toll on me. I was exhausted, the blankets were the best thing I'd slept on since the Vipers took me, and the steady patter of rain against the roof was enough to lure me into a doze. With nothing better to do, I closed my eyes and let myself drift off to sleep.

The crackling fire sent embers swirling up in the air. They were bright against the darkness, like tiny golden stars. I played with my hair, twirling one blue lock around my finger as I watched the embers dance lazily over the fire. "I see you're still keeping up with that I'm-a-serial-killer storyline, hmm?"

Ethan shot me an incredulous look. "It's the truth."

I shrugged, studying him from across the fire, laid out as he was with one arm tucked under his head. He was so tall that it was hard to study his face closely most of the time, but with him lying down I could make out the small scar on his cheek, the faint stubble on his jaw, the green in his hazel eyes. The firelight illuminated the lighter hues of his blonde hair where it fell in waves across his forehead.

For someone who claimed to be a serial killer, he was ridiculously good-looking, in a rugged, rough-hewn kind of way.

It was funny to tease him. It's not that I didn't believe him, as crazy of a story as it was. He didn't strike me as the type to make up a lie like that. And his mannerisms certainly supported his claim, everything from his grumpy aloofness to his permanent glare. But since poking fun at Ethan had become my new favorite pastime, I smiled at him and said, "I just find it hard to believe."

"Do you think I just made all of that up?" he demanded.

"You've had days to think up a story."

He groaned. "I'm telling the truth."

I flashed him a saccharine-sweet smile. "Sure you are."

Ethan shook his head, and I caught a flash of a smile while his head was turned.

A smile.

I gasped dramatically. "What's wrong with your face? That couldn't be a smile, could it?" I started laughing, and Ethan averted his gaze, his mouth a quivering line as he tried to rein the expression in. I grinned. "Is it possible for the brooding assassin to crack a smile?"

"I don't know what you're talking about," he ground out.

"He's smiling." I could dance with joy. "I finally did it. I accomplished my life's goal of making you smile. My work here is complete, so you're on your own now."

I was only half kidding. I was used to people being annoyed with me, but Ethan took it to another level. Hell, he was annoyed with everything. Always walking around with this stony expression, not quite a scowl but far from neutral, his eyes narrowing dangerously every time I opened up my mouth. I wasn't fully convinced that someone hadn't put a spell on him, forcing him into a permanent bad mood.

But I'd finally gotten the big grump to smile.

Ethan refused to look me in the eye, even though he was grinning now. "You're impossible."

I grinned and poked him in the arm. "He's smiling, he's smiling, he's—"

"Wake up."

My eyes flew open, the memory evaporating. I grasped at the scraps, Ethan trying and failing to hide a grin while I teased him about it. That had been such a fun night, the first time I felt like we understood each other. The first time I actually felt like his *friend* rather than the girl tagging along and annoying him to high heaven. Something had shifted between us that night, and I would have done anything to have that feeling back.

But it was Josh who stood over me now, nudging my shoulder with his boot, much harder than necessary. "Wake up," he said again, his irritation clear. I sat up with a sigh as the memory floated away. It was probably for the best, given my vow to stop thinking about Ethan.

Even if my dreams had other ideas.

I noticed the handcuffs had been unlocked, leaving me free to stand up. Josh had brought reinforcements this time, two Vipers I didn't recognize. Troy was gone, the swivel chair sitting empty in the corner of the room.

"The boss wants to see you," Josh said.

F O U R

Nico held court in what once was a dining hall. A massive metal table dominated the space, an odd collection of mismatched chairs surrounding it. The double doors leading inside hadn't escaped the onslaught of graffiti, the word *COMMAND* painted out in the red paint Nico used at the church and the house by the ocean. The inside of the room was covered in the same gruesome murals that adorned the rest of the building. The windows were boarded up, not even offering the smallest sliver of light. Instead the room was lit by a series of battery-operated lanterns, their harsh white glow blinding me from where they sat on the table.

The man himself lounged at the head of the table like a dark king presiding over his subjects. There was no amusement in his eyes like there had been before. No mirth, no wicked delight. Just cold, unrelenting focus.

He was done playing games.

"Sit down," he ordered.

Josh shoved me into the chair opposite Nico, the two of us studying each other from across the metal table. Ren sat to the left of Nico. Josh took the seat to the right, Troy appearing beside him. The other Vipers claimed the remaining seats. I glanced at each of them, searching for a sign of hope, a potential ally, but all I found were unfriendly gazes. Thunder rumbled in the distance, making the hairs on the back of my neck stand up.

"I want to know where the giant is," Nico said, his voice cold.

"Ethan," I snapped.

He raised a brow.

"Ethan," I said louder. "His name is Ethan. Not *the giant,* not *the big oaf.*" I glared at them. "*Ethan.*"

"Fine." He propped his legs up on the table. "Tell me where *Ethan* is."

"I don't know," I said flatly.

"You have to know."

My jaw clenched. "I'm afraid I don't. We had a fight and he took off. He could be on the other side of the country by now, for all I know. But it doesn't matter, because I know he doesn't care enough to come back for me."

Nico clicked his tongue. "I think you underestimate his feelings for you."

I snorted. "No, I *over*estimated them. He's gone. He's not coming for me." I choked a little on the words. "This whole game you're playing is useless. Just let me go."

His eyes narrowed as he studied me. He exchanged a dark look with Josh and Ren, who both shrugged. There was no way for them to know if I was telling the truth or not, even if I thought Ethan's absence thus far was plenty of evidence.

"Don't keep this up," I begged. "This plan isn't going to work because Ethan doesn't care about me enough for me to be good bait. If he's the one you've got a problem with, then you don't need me. Find another way to go after him and just let me go. Or if you're going to—" I stuttered. "If you're going to get rid of me, then hurry up and do it. Don't make me wait."

The room fell quiet. The Vipers exchanged a look. Ren shifted in his seat. Nico tilted his head thoughtfully.

"She's lying."

I didn't recognize the Viper who spoke, a woman with chestnut hair and amber eyes, one of two females here besides me. Nico seemed to genuinely consider her words. I had a feeling that everyone at this table bore some sort of importance to him. Perhaps these Vipers formed some kind of mock Council, a group to decide the inner workings of their gang.

Another murmured, "Then why isn't the giant here yet? Aren't they always together? Why is he missing?"

"This could be a trap," a different Viper theorized.

"Does that mean the giant's coming?"

"We should get rid of the girl."

"The boss has a plan for her—"

"What if—"

"I don't think—"

"But—"

"If—"

"I—"

The meeting dissolved into a buzz of voices. Nico was the only one who remained quiet, his eyes darting back and forth, following the volley of words with the air of someone watching an interesting sports match. He caught me looking and smiled, even as his people began to rise from their seats, their voices raising to screams and shouts.

I'd gotten the impression that the Vipers were like a well-oiled machine. They seemed to work so well together before. But the moment there was a disagreement, they defaulted to petty arguments. Interesting. I didn't know much about the real Council, but I had a feeling they were at least civil with each other.

"Enough!" Nico boomed.

The room fell silent. Nico raked a scathing glare over all of them. "Keep your voices down," he demanded. "I wanted your presence, not your opinions." A few ducked their heads, a-shamed. "We aren't going to let the girl go," he continued, to the quiet outrage of a few Vipers. He ignored them. "She might be telling the truth, but I think the giant will be back. He'll look for her eventually, and when he does…" Nico shrugged. "We'll be ready."

"But how long is that going to take?" Troy asked. "How long are we going to wait?"

"As long as necessary," Nico said, ice creeping into his tone. He nodded at me. "Ren, take her back to the cell. She doesn't get any food until she's willing to give us some in-formation. She at least has to know what direction he went in. The minute she's willing to spill, she can have a meal. Until then she can go hungry."

I did, in fact, know which direction Ethan went in, but as mad as I was at him, I wasn't about to sell him out to a bunch of bloodthirsty rogues and exiles. I held Nico's gaze as Ren pulled me from my seat. He smirked, waving a mocking hand in farewell.

Ren marched me back down the hall in silence. I snuck a glance at him. His jaw was set, his eyes focused firmly ahead. If I was going to find an ally in this place, I thought Ren would be my best chance—he was one of Nico's closest people, it seemed, but he was also the only one that had presented any kind of a moral compass.

And it didn't hurt that he was scared to death of Ethan. There had to be a way to use that to my advantage.

I was returned to the cell and handcuffed to the bar. Ren claimed Troy's chair with much more dignity than its former occupant. He pulled a small book out of his back pocket. It was a battered paperback novel, the front cover too creased to make out the title, though the cowboy on the front suggested it was a western.

A smile twitched on my lips. Ren was a reader. He sensed me staring and fixed me with a stern glare until I dropped my gaze.

I laid back down. I wasn't tired enough to sleep anymore, so I laid there in silence, the rustle of turning pages the only sound in the room. The handcuff was beginning to hurt my wrist. My clothes were dirty from days of travel, my tank top still bearing a bloodstain from a mutant I killed days ago. My skin was covered in dirt and grime, itching all over, and I found myself desperately wishing for a bath.

I said as much to Ren, who told me without looking up, "There's no running water here. We rinse off in a creek behind the building, but there's no way we're risking that." He turned the page. "You'll just have to get used to it."

We didn't speak for another three hours.

There was no window in the room to judge the time by, but I suspected it was nighttime. This was usually when I would pop outside for a little while, anything from a minute to a couple hours, and stare up at the night sky sprinkled with glittering stars.

My free hand drifted up to my broken heart necklace. I missed Lucy, missed sneaking outside every night with her.

I propped myself up on one elbow. "I have a request."

Ren ripped his eyes away from the book. "I told you, we don't have a shower."

"I want to see the stars."

He blinked. "Why?" He shook his head. "Actually, never mind. It doesn't matter because I can't do it."

"I don't care if it's outside or through a window. Just take me somewhere I can see the sky, even if it's just for a minute." Ren bit his lip, and I pushed. "I'm not trying to escape. It's just that my sister and I always used to go out and watch the stars. She lives in the Houston Safe Zone. I haven't seen her in two years, but every night I go out and look up so I can see the same stars she does and not feel alone." My voice cracked. "Please."

Ren held my gaze for a long moment.

"Five minutes," he said.

Relief flooded through me. Ren tossed the book onto the cabinet and unlocked the handcuffs. I rubbed my sore wrist as he escorted me down the darkened halls, using the beam of a flashlight to illuminate the way.

"We've got guards at every door," he said to me, his strides long and confident. He no doubt knew this place like the back of his hand, even in the dark. "We can't go outside, not with the boss on high alert because of your friend. But I can get you to a window."

We emerged in what looked like a rec room. It was late enough that nobody was in there, a shelf of puzzles and board games left abandoned. Ren strode past it to a wide window on the far wall. It squealed like a pig when he shoved it open. I smiled at the night air that greeted me with a cool kiss.

Ren poked his head out the window. "The rain has cleared up, but there's still some clouds." He glanced at me over his shoulder. "You're going to be disappointed if you were wanting to see much."

"I don't need a lot." I crossed over to the window. Ren was right; thick clouds obscured most of the sky, but my eyes searched out the tiny sliver of inky sky, a smattering of bright stars just visible. I fingered my necklace as I took a seat in the windowsill. The smell of rain and fresh earth was thick and welcoming. I loved the scent. It smelled like nature.

I realized Ren still stood behind me, his expression unreadable. He switched off the flashlight and took a seat next to me.

"It's kinda freaky that you smile so much," he said.

I glanced at him. "Is there something wrong with that?"

He shrugged. "Not particularly. It's just that you're…" He cringed. "My boss kidnapped you, and that's liable to make a person mad, but instead you're smiling, and if I'm being honest it's kind of giving me the creeps."

The words came out in a rush, as if he was embarrassed to say them. I snorted. "I'm smiling because there is something making me happy." The after-rain scent wrapped around me as I leaned out the window, enjoying the breeze against my flushed skin. "I love this."

Ren stared out the window for a few moments.

"I can see why you like it," he admitted quietly.

I nodded. "It's peaceful. And it reminds me of my sister."

He tilted his head. "Was she nice?" he asked. "Your sister?"

"Nice?" I laughed under my breath. "Lord a'mercy. She wasn't *nice*; she was the best."

He smiled softly. "It's cool to have someone like that. I never did. My whole family died when I was three. I was exiled at seventeen for stealing food, been out here ever since. The Vipers were the best thing that ever happened to me."

"How so?"

"Groups are the key to survival. There's safety in numbers. I have a roof over my head because of these people, plenty of food and supplies, too." He shrugged. "Nico can be an asshole, sure, but he's given me a purpose."

"Nico isn't the one who gives you that," I said quietly. "The man upstairs is. And I know He wouldn't approve of what Nico does."

"I don't believe in God," Ren said, a little forcefully.

He was defensive. I pressed on. "You don't have to in order to know this is wrong. You seem like a good guy. There is better than this—better people, better groups. Better *lives*." I paused. "I think you know that."

His eyes went distant. "You don't know anything about me."

I planted a hand on my hip. "I know you think this is wrong."

Ren flinched.

"It's never too late to do the right thing," I said, my voice as gentle as I could make it. "You can let me go, then come with me to find a better life." I could see the war of emotion in his eyes. I laid a hand on his arm. "You are the one who gets to choose that. What Nico orders you to do doesn't matter."

At the mention of his boss' name, Ren's eyes went cold. He yanked his arm away, stumbling from the window. "I don't have to, but I want to. I trust Nico."

"That's a lie."

"Bold words coming from a prisoner."

He would have done better to slap me across the face. I shot to my feet. "Ren—"

"Don't pretend to know me," he hissed. "You're just trying to get in my head, but it's not going to work." He slammed the window shut. "Your time is up. Let's go."

"But—"

"Let's go," he snapped.

His expression was cold as stone, an unfeeling mask. I had been so close. I had almost convinced him.

But almost wasn't enough.

I dropped my head. Ren flipped on the flashlight and took my arm, his grip firmer than it was before. I let him lead me back to the cell, let him cuff my arm. He disappeared through the door; a few minutes later, a new Viper appeared to take over watch, a burly bloke with beady eyes and a thick jaw. Ren came in long enough to collect his book. He refused to look at me as he stalked out.

I looked at my new guard. His eyes narrowed. "Don't say a word," he ground out, his voice so thick I could hardly understand him.

I sighed and slumped against the blankets as I fought back a fresh round of tears.

FIVE

The next two days passed in a blur. I spent most of it sprawled out on the blanket, ready to claw off my skin if it meant I could be clean. After my conversation with Ren, I found it hard to sleep, every noise and breath keeping me awake. There was no more going to look at the stars. The only thing I was allowed to look at was the inside of this makeshift cell, with the graffiti on its walls and its lack of a window. My racing thoughts were only rivaled by the growing pain in my stomach. I couldn't remember the last time I'd eaten—sometime before I came to the base. That was days ago.

The only source of entertainment I had was in the form of a pen I found stashed beneath the pile of blankets. The clip had long since broken off, but there was still ink in it. After a disastrous attempt to pick the lock to the handcuffs using the pen, I resorted to doodling on the walls and floor, drawing little flowers and stick figures and landscapes until the ink ran dry.

I had the vaguest memory of the guards changing out every couple of hours. They were all new faces, nameless and cruel, smirking down at me. I turned away, cradling my cuffed arm and wishing, *begging* for everything to end.

I missed my church. I missed my home in Houston. I missed Lucy. I missed Ethan.

Bull. Oh, I missed him. There was no way I could lie to myself about it anymore. I wished he would show up with his knives flashing and murder in his eyes like there had been when those two Vipers found us in the woods. If he had been with me, Nico would have never been able to take me. One look from *the giant* had them quaking in their boots.

It hurt to think about him. I had been so convinced he was better than Avery. Avery, who had been an asshole from the start. Had it not been for his interest in my appearance disguised as genuine care, had it not been for my parents wanting me to pair up with someone who worked in the government, I never would have ended up with him. Lucy and I seemed to be the only ones to see right through him. But I tried to make it work for my parents' sake. I thought they saw something I didn't.

But the memory of that day was crystal-clear in my mind. The town had been having a summer cook-out to celebrate Independence Day. Avery and his friends had too much to drink. Jesse Dawson had gotten into a fight with Avery over something—what, I didn't know—and the two were on the verge of a drunken brawl in the center of town. I grabbed Avery's arm and tugged him into the shadow of a nearby building to coax him out of it. I hadn't gotten but three words in when he slapped me across the face. My head rocked to the side and pain exploded across my cheek. *Get out of my way, bitch,* Avery spat before stalking away.

I had stood there, dumbfounded, for a full five minutes before reality crashed into me. I burst into tears and ran all the way home. After locking myself in my room, I sat on the end of my bed with a pillow hugged against my chest, attempting to sort my racing thoughts. I wanted to talk but didn't know who to turn to. Nobody had seen it. Lucy would believe me, but I'd seen her partying with her friends and I hated to ruin her day.

Hours passed. Then a knock came at the door. I expected it to be Lucy, coming to check on me, but when I opened my bedroom door, it was Avery who stood there, his red hair mused and his amber eyes dark.

We need to talk, he said.

We sure do, I replied.

I thought he had come to apologize for slapping me. But he pretended it never happened. He ranted about embarrassing him in front of his friends by pulling him aside and acting like I was his boss. He told me I was an awful girlfriend, and if it wasn't for how pretty I was, he would have dumped me long ago. I stared at him in disbelief for a few minutes while he talked, and then I made a decision it wouldn't happen anymore.

I told him we were over. He was an asshole, I never had liked him, and we were *done.* We argued and screamed until the neighbors beat on the door and said they'd call in soldiers if we kept on. Avery hadn't seemed keen on keeping quiet, so I told him to leave. When it became clear he had no intention of doing so, I tried to shove him out the door.

I hadn't seen the knife until I felt a sharp pain in my abdomen and looked down to see the hilt still in Avery's hand.

One of these days, he snarled, *you will learn not to push me.*

And then he walked out the door as I collapsed.

Lucy arrived a few minutes later, a smile dying on her lips when she found me. Having trained at the hospital to become a nurse, she was able to stitch me up. Her blue eyes went cold when I told her what happened.

He's not going to get away with this, she said, squeezing my hand. *I'm going to the guard post to tell them about this. Just hang tight.*

She was gone and back within ten minutes. Alarm bells went off as I took in her pale face, the anger in her eyes. Lucy was a passionate person, but it was rare for her to be *furious*, and that was the only word that could describe her expression.

What happened? I demanded.

We have to get out of here.

Why?

Avery beat me there. He said a mutant got into the compound and bit you. The soldiers are coming to put you down, Laiken.

I didn't question her, not when there was pure terror in her eyes. She grabbed my hand and pulled me through the back exit just as the front door was kicked down. We ran as fast as my injury would allow, not stopping until we were at the gates.

You need to leave, Lucy told me, her words breathless and panicked. *Avery wants the truth dead so he can uphold his reputation.* Her face twisted with disgust. *You are going to hide in the wastelands for a couple weeks, then head to a different Safe Zone and seek refuge. You'll be gone long enough to prove you're perfectly healthy, no mutant bites. But go to Austin or Dallas—don't come back here. I don't want you anywhere near that prick again.*

But—

No buts, Laiken. He wants you dead. *I won't let him touch my baby sister.*

She took her necklace and fitted it with mine, forming the full hurt.

We'll both keep our necklaces on, and every night we can go and look at the same stars and know the other is okay. You are going to be okay, *Laiken. I know it.* Her blue eyes, twin to mine, searched my face. *Just two weeks or so, then you can seek refuge in Austin or Dallas and write me a letter from there.*

Are you sure? I whispered.

Lucy pulled me into a tight hug. *No,* she whispered back. *But these soldiers will shoot before they check to see if you were really bitten. You need to run.* She released me. *Now.*

And so, with a plan concocted under the moonlight of a warm summer night, I slipped through the gates after Lucy flirted one of the guards into opening them. She threw together a bag of supplies and squeezed me into another bone-crushing hug before whispering, *See you soon.*

That had been two years ago.

Did it make me a coward, that I was too scared to go back? Probably. Lucy no doubt thought I was dead.

It was better this way. Nobody else in Houston liked me. Nobody in the *wastelands* liked me.

I wished somebody was here. I wanted Ethan. He would have a plan.

I really had thought he was different. That he wouldn't hurt me like Avery had. And while Ethan had never laid a hand on me, never injured me physically, this felt worse somehow.

Even now, I still thought he was a good guy deep down, a diamond in the rough like I told him. There was a kind soul buried under all that stony indifference. But if he refused to show it, then it didn't matter if it was there or not.

I was vaguely aware of the door opening, of the murmured voices of guards exchanging posts. I laid facing the wall, dead-eyed and tired, wishing there was someone who cared enough to at least let me clean up. There was the creak of the chair as the newcomer sat down, the snick of the door closing behind the last guard. I squeezed my eyes shut.

"You don't have to look so depressed."

That voice. My head whipped to the side to see Nico lounging in the chair. His dark hair was combed to the side, his clothes fresh and his skin clean. He crossed one ankle over his knee and smiled at my discomfort.

"It's been a while since we've talked," he drawled. "And it's been a few days since you've eaten. I thought I might see if you were willing to give me some information."

"I don't have information," I snapped, even as my stomach growled. Lord a'*mercy*, I was hungry. It felt as if there was a beast attempting to claw its way out of my stomach. I'd gone hungry the first few weeks in the wastelands after Lucy's supplies ran out, but once I stumbled across the church, food and supplies were no longer a problem.

Nico sensed my distress, and his smile widened. "Come on, sweetheart. I know you're hungry. I have a pretty good cook in my group. I'm sure she'll be more than happy to make you something, if only you would give us a teeny bit of information about the giant. Just give me *something*. I know he can't be gone for good."

"Well, he is."

"You're lying."

"Am I? Tell me this, then—why wasn't Ethan at the church? Why hasn't he shown up already? *He doesn't care about me.* He's not coming, like I have told you a thousand times."

Nico tilted his head, his dark hair slipping over his brow. "What makes you so sure? I know how to read an expression, sweetheart, and the look on the giant's face told me everything I needed to know." The corners of his lips ticked up. "He'll come. And we'll be waiting for him when he does."

"You're wrong," I said. Nico hadn't been there when we fought. When I screamed at Ethan to leave and he took off without a backwards glance. He didn't know our history.

Ethan wasn't coming for me.

Nobody was.

My chest tightened, making it hard to breathe. Nico noted my expression with raised brows and opened his mouth to say something, but he was cut off by a pounding on the door.

"Come in," he snapped.

The door swung open, revealing Josh, Ren, and an unfamiliar Viper. His pale face had me tensing. Josh and Ren bore stone-cold expressions, their eyes grim.

Something happened.

"We have trouble, boss," Josh said gravely. He nudged the other Viper. "Tell him."

He gulped. "I found Troy in the hall." He dropped his gaze. "His throat's been slit."

The air whooshed out of me. Troy, the one who'd taken such pride in destroying my church. The one who had spun the swivel chair around like a little kid when he was supposed to be guarding me.

He was dead?

Nico's eyes narrowed as he stood up. "Who did it?"

Ren shook his head. "No one's seen him. The guards out back are MIA." He grimaced. "He's in here somewhere."

He.

Lord a'mercy.

Nico turned to face me with a smile so cold it sent a shiver down my spine.

"Well, sweetheart," he crooned, "it looks like the giant came after all."

SIX

The giant came after all.

Nico pulled me down the hall and into the command room. He barked orders to every Viper that passed, telling his men to gather outside the doors. I was trembling so hard I barely noticed as he passed me off to Josh and Ren. The pair shoved me into the chair at the head of the table—the same chair Nico had sat in like a throne a couple days ago—and tied my wrists and ankles down with thick rope. A single lantern was set on the edge of the table, blinding me with harsh white light.

Ethan. He was here.

It had to be him, right? Who else could it be? I listened through the open doors as more Vipers appeared, reporting bodies found in the hallway. Nico had been smiling at first, but now his expression was serious as he organized his men.

His few men, I noted with both horror and satisfaction. There weren't even ten people now. He had at least thirty before.

But every report that came in said the same—just a body on the floor, a pool of blood on the ground. No sign of the attacker. Not a trace of the person they refused to talk about in anything other than a whisper.

It had to be Ethan. He was an *assassin*. This was what he did for a living. But a voice in the back of my mind whispered that it could easily be someone else, perhaps another gang that Nico had ticked off or even a Viper with a grievance.

I heard one Viper telling his companion it was like a ghost had entered their complex. It didn't seem possible that someone as big as Ethan could remain undetected for so long, not when he was barely able to walk in my church without knocking a hundred things over. I knew he was good at what he did, but was he *this* good?

My breathing picked up its pace, my heart kicking into high gear. I wanted so desperately for it to be him. I *needed* it to be him.

Josh gave an experimental tug to the ropes holding me down. "She's secure, boss."

Nico flashed a thumbs-up and continued to rattle off orders.

Josh exchanged a dark look with Ren. "I'm going to help. You've got her?"

He nodded, and Josh took off to stand at Nico's side. Ren shuffled on his feet, his finger curling around the trigger of his rifle.

I had one last opportunity to convince him.

"You still have the chance to end this," I said to him. "It's not too late."

"Shut up."

The words were harsh. I flinched. "Ren, I'm telling you, if that really is Ethan out there—"

"If it really is him, then he's going to die. Now shut up."

"I'm trying to save your life!" I exploded. "Can't you see that? However the chips fall, this is going to be bloody. I—"

"*Shut up!*" he roared.

The words echoed off the walls. I shrunk back, stung.

"Is there a problem?" Nico thundered from the doorway.

Ren shot me one last glare before turning to his boss. "Nope."

"Good." He and Josh sauntered into the room, kicking the doors shut, trapping the four of us inside. "Now all we do is wait."

"How long do you think it will take?" Ren asked.

"I don't know. The giant will find us eventually. We're already really low on numbers—he's been picking us off one by one, and I think a few have taken off on their own, the cowards." He spat on the ground. "But he can't kill us all at once, so when he tries, we'll have the advantage."

His eyes gleamed. This was all a game to him, his people nothing more than pawns. He didn't care how many lives were lost, how much blood was spilled, even if it was his own people dying.

"You're a sick man," I said, my voice laced with barely-concealed fury. "And a horrible leader."

Nico shot me a glare. Ren pinched the bridge of his nose. "Be quiet," Josh ordered.

"No."

Nico's eyes narrowed. "What did you just say?"

"I said no." My voice rose higher. "You don't care about your own people. You're willing to let them die just so you can carry out your grudge and protect your pride. That is not a quality of a good person, much less a good leader."

"I'd advise you to close your mouth, sweetheart."

"Stop calling me that."

"Then stop running your damn mouth!" Ren snapped.

"I guess we're not even going to mention all of the kidnapping," I continued, just as loud. "Using a woman as bait? That is sick and degrading and cowardly. A horrible move, too, if you ask me. You—"

"I said, *be quiet*," Nico snarled, shoving his gun against my temple. I sucked in a breath as the cool metal bit against my skin. "Quiet!" he panted, eyes wild.

I glared up at him. "I hope Ethan kills you all."

Nico bared his teeth. "You filthy bitc—"

The deafening roar of gunfire drowned out the rest of the word. His head snapped to the double doors. I didn't dare move with the gun so close. The gunfire ceased, replaced by shouting and the slap of footsteps against the ground.

"What the hell was that?" Josh asked, voice low.

"Maybe they found him," Ren said, just as quietly.

The voice and footsteps faded—they were giving chase. My throat tightened.

"They better bring me his head," Nico growled.

He circled around me, gripping my shoulder hard enough to bruise and keeping the gun glued to my temple. Ren and Josh fell back to either side of him, gripping their rifles until their knuckles turned white.

More shots rang out, deeper inside the building. Nico tensed as silence reigned. I realized I was holding my breath.

It was a deadly kind of quiet, the kind that made your heart rate erratic and caused you to jump at every breath. I could only pray Nico's trigger finger wasn't as tense as the hand on my shoulder was.

Minutes ticked by. I forced myself to suck in a breath and let it out. Again. Again. A—

The door handle rattled.

The three Vipers and I watched as the handle moved up and down. The door was locked so it didn't open, leaving the three of us in a breathless silence as the only sound in the room was the rattling of the handle.

It stopped moving. Nico exhaled a long breath, loosening his grip on my shoulder. I relaxed, just a touch.

Then there was a loud crash. The doors flew inwards, smacking against the walls like two claps of thunder.

My heart stuttered as the lone figure appeared in the doorway. A bloody knife was in one hand, a pistol in the other. World-ending rage flickered in his hazel eyes. The front of his t-shirt was soaked with blood, a splatter of crimson on his face. His dark blonde hair was a sweat-slicked mess, plastered to his forehead in damp waves. The harsh lantern-light cast deep shadows on his face as he surveyed Ren and Josh and Nico in turn. His eyes narrowed as he took in their weapons.

And then Ethan looked at me, and I couldn't help the sob that cracked through me.

He came.

He came.

"Why don't you sit down?" Nico said. Shadows fell across his face as he angled his head, fixing Ethan with a sharp smile. "I believe we have some negotiating to do."

Ethan yielded one step, his gaze sweeping across the room, assessing the situation. Ren and Josh shuffled nervously under the weight of his gaze.

Then he looked at me, really looked, taking in every scrape and stain and bruise. He noted the ropes holding my wrists in place with a slight tic of his jaw, and when he returned his gaze to Nico, it was even colder than before.

"You've been quite busy, haven't you?" Nico asked. "I've had a lot of reports from my people that they've found their comrades dead on the floor."

"The reporters are dead too."

Ethan's voice was soft, but there was a lethal undertone that made Nico flinch. The pistol dug into my head. "I have a proposition. I'll let the girl go if you turn yourself in."

What? I stared at Ethan, silently begging him not to negotiate with this maniac. "Like you would keep your word," he snapped.

Nico seethed. "You seem to have a tactic you favor for killing my men, don't you? You wait until they are alone before you strike." He waved a hand at me, and Ethan's eyes iced over. "I found her alone, and it was the opportune moment. I regret nothing from my previous actions concerning the two of you except that I didn't go about it the right way." He smirked. "All I had to do was find your weakness."

Weakness.

I froze.

I cannot have you making me weak.

Caring for someone is not a weakness. What you did back there wasn't wrong. You are not weak, Ethan.

I was. But you're right: I'm not weak. Not anymore.

What does that mean? Bull! What does that mean?

It means I'm leaving.

I stared at Ethan. His gaze dropped down to mine, his hazel eyes hard. I wondered if he was remembering that same conversation, the words echoing in his head like they did mine. His expression was as unreadable as always as he stood on the other side of the table with an unearthly stillness.

Ethan looked back up at Nico.

And then he growled, "She's not a weakness."

SEVEN

I choked on another sob, tears streaming down my cheeks. I wanted nothing more in that moment than to run to him, to throw my arms around him and laugh with joy and relief.

But Nico ruined the moment. "She told us that you had left and weren't coming back," he said. "Days passed, and I almost thought she was right. I even lightened up on some of my patrols. Another day or two, and I would have called off the thing entirely and killed the little sweetheart."

His hand stroked my hair. I shivered, and Ethan noted the movement with narrowed eyes. Nico laughed under his breath. "But, here you are. Furious, and rightly so, I suppose. I kidnapped your woman and took your stuff. That's liable to make any man mad, isn't it?"

Ethan sucked in a breath. "The majority of your men are dead. If you think you're going to get out of this much better, then think again."

He just laughed. "Big talk for a big guy. Face the facts, you big oaf: I have the girl at gunpoint, and there is nothing you can do from over there that can stop me from pulling this trigger."

He raised a brow. "The person behind you might."

Nico and the others whirled around. I wished I could see who the newcomer was, but then Ethan slid forward a few feet and Nico whirled around with a snarl.

"I got you," Ethan said, his tone mocking. A trick—that's all it had been. "Now, what would have happened if I had my gun ready and I shot you in the head right then?" He held up his pistol. "You underestimate me."

Dangerous, lethal words. Ethan's eyes burned with icy intensity. I wondered how anyone dared stand up to him—if it were me in Nico's position, I would have already run for the hills.

"You have one minute," Nico breathed. "One minute to decide: Do you want to turn yourself in and let the girl live, or let her die and you walk away free?"

"Lay another hand on her," he snarled, "and I will cut off that hand."

The gun pressed against my temple, drawing a sharp breath out of me. Ethan's eyes met mine for a brief moment before flicking away again, surveying the room. I watched his jaw clench.

He was trying to figure out a plan.

I struggled to control my breathing.

But then Ethan glanced at me again and rocked back on his heels. The movement was so quick I nearly missed it. He did it again a second later, and I realized he wanted me to copy him. But I couldn't—

Wait a damn second.

I glanced at Nico, at his position relative to my chair. I tested my legs. The ropes around my ankles weren't as tight as the ones holding my wrists down, granting me just enough room to put my feet flat on the floor.

I looked up and gave Ethan the barest of nods.

I could have sworn a ghost of a smile flitted over his face as he turned to Nico. "I surrender."

Nico grinned. "Smart move, giant."

Ethan held out his pistol and knife, slowly lowering them to the floor. In the corners of my vision, I saw Ren and Josh's rifles tracking his movement. I pressed my feet flat against the floor, my muscles tense as I stretched my legs as much as my bindings would allow me.

"*Now!*" Ethan roared, disappearing under the table.

Gunfire thundered on either side of me. I slammed my feet into the floor. My chair rocked back, taking me with it, and I felt a thump as the back of the chair slammed right into Nico's stomach. The gun vanished from my temple. But I had pushed a little too hard, and with my hands tied down, there was nothing I could do to stop the chair from rocking all the way back.

I slammed into the ground with a grunt, my head cracking against the floor. My vision went dark; for a brief, horrible moment I thought I had hit my head so hard I'd blinded myself, but then I realized the lantern had gone dark. The beam of a flashlight cut through the room, followed by more gunshots, but then everything went dark and quiet. Somewhere to my left, I heard someone moaning in pain. My mind spun as I tried to remember who had been on that side of the room before, but my thoughts were a chaotic mess.

I didn't dare call Ethan's name.

A voice called from my right, "That was a clever trick."

Nico.

"Why don't you talk to me?" he asked. "Don't you want to explain yourself? Don't you want to tell me why it took you so long to rescue your damsel in distress?" His voice moved further away. "She seemed *certain* you were out of the picture, and it's hard to fake that kind of emotion. Did you know she was crying when he found her?" He laughed, and it took everything I had not to shriek at the sound of his cold laugh in the dark room. "Oh, yeah. She was bawling her eyes out."

The person next to me moaned again. I couldn't figure out who it was. Panic set it and I clamped my mouth shut, my head throbbing from where I'd smacked it on the ground.

Ethan—

"He's here! He's here! He's—"

The voice beside me rose to a scream, and I realized it was Ren. But he was soon drowned out by several shots firing, bullets pinging off the metal table. One whooshed by my ear, and I let out a little scream that was drowned out by the gunfire.

The sound ceased. Ren wasn't moaning anymore. I let out a low whimper as I bit down on my lip hard enough to draw blood.

"Where did you go?" Nico taunted. "Come on, giant, we just want to talk. I have a deal for you."

His voice edged closer now. I gripped the arms of the chair, trying to keep myself together. I'd only read one horror novel in my lifetime, but this was starting to feel a lot like the beginnings of one.

A hand fell on my leg. I nearly screamed, but another hand covered my mouth.

"Quiet," Ethan breathed, his lips brushing my ear.

Oh, God. He was alive. He gave my knee a light squeeze, his calloused fingers warm against my clammy skin, and I grounded myself in the touch before he was gone. Now that I knew what to listen for, I could hear the faint sound of him breathing somewhere next to me.

Something clattered in the distance. I didn't quite catch what happened next, but suddenly there was a bright flash of light and three shots fired. My eyes adjusted just in time to see

Ethan's tall form storming across the room. The table blocked most of my view, but I saw Josh on the ground, Nico doubled over in front of him, blood dripping from a wound in his stomach. He didn't have time to react before Ethan was on him, one large hand grabbing his throat and slamming him against the wall. Ethan tossed his flashlight on the table and pressed his pistol against Nico's forehead.

"Are you happy now?" he snarled. His breathing was ragged, his fingers digging into Nico's tan throat. "All the times I warned you to stay away from me, all the times that you tried again and again to get me because I made you mad and you thought you could get your revenge." Nico let out a weak cough as Ethan crushed his windpipe. His clawed weakly at Ethan's hand, a valiant effort.

Ethan leaned right into his face and yelled, "*How did it work out for you?*"

I gasped at the sudden rise in his tone. Our little fight didn't seem quite so bad now, not when I realized I hadn't even seen the tip of Ethan's wrath.

Nico gave him a slow, bloody smile.

"You're clever, I'll give you that," he rasped. His voice grew weaker with every word. "A worthy opponent. But I know I'm right about you leaving the girl. I can recognize a genuine feeling when I see one, and the look in your eyes…" His laugh sent another tremor down my spine. "You came here out of guilt, didn't you?"

I couldn't see Ethan's expression, but I saw his shoulders tense. He tossed Nico to the ground like he weighed nothing, the air whooshing out of him as Ethan's steel-toed boot stomped down on his chest.

"So what do you plan to do now?" Nico wheezed. "Kill me? Will it make you feel better for leaving her?"

The fight had turned enough for me to catch the fury glinting in Ethan's eyes.

"There isn't a thing in this world that would make me feel better for leaving her," he said, kneeling down on top of him. "*Nothing.*"

A tear slipped down my cheek.

Nico panted. "Then it's not too late to stop. You can let me go, and I'll never bother you again, because I know you'll be busy patching things up with her." He coughed. "She's pretty, but you know that already, right? If you hadn't come I might have been tempted to take her myself."

He coughed again. Ethan's jaw ticked, and I realized Nico had said the wrong damn thing.

"But I swear it, giant," he wheezed, blood gleaming on his teeth. "You let me go, and you will never have to see my face again."

"Just because I said nothing would make me feel better about leaving Laiken," he breathed, "doesn't mean killing you won't be extremely satisfying." His finger tightened on the trigger of his gun. "I killed the rest of your men. What made you think I would stop before I got to their leader?"

Nico stared at him, his dark eyes clashing with Ethan's hazel ones.

"Make it quick," he whispered. "I don't want to suffer."

A beat of silence.

Ethan studied him for a long moment. "You'll suffer enough as it is."

And he pulled the trigger.

The gunshot shattered the air. A pool of blood formed under Nico's head as Ethan stumbled to his feet, retreating several steps. His breathing was ragged, his eyes weary. He stared and stared and stared at Nico's body as if he couldn't quite believe it. He stared for so long that I was worried he was about to use the gun for something else.

"Ethan?" I asked.

He snapped out of his trance, whirling around to face me. We stared at each other from across the room, his expression as unreadable as always.

"You came back for me," I sobbed.

EIGHT

Ethan's expression shattered. He crashed to his knees next to me, heartbreak and pain and grief on his face, perhaps the most emotion I'd ever seen him show. "I'm sorry," he breathed, tripping over the words. "I tried to come back, to talk to you, but when I got to the church—"

He cut himself off. The look in his eyes told me that he'd seen enough of the church to piece together what happened. I closed my eyes. "They destroyed it. Nico made me watch. He managed to track me—"

"I'm sorry."

I opened my eyes to look at him. "It's not your fault they came for me. Not at all." He opened his mouth to argue, so I forged ahead, "I was angry, so angry with you after you left. Nico's right: I did cry, more than I have in a long time. I thought you weren't going to come back, and that upset me. What upset me even more is when Nico and his Vipers came into the church and I realized you weren't there to protect me, because *damn*, Bull, it sure is handy having a literal giant following you around. I stayed locked up in the church before you came along because I knew I couldn't handle myself if I got involved with a dangerous group."

The truth came pouring out, and I couldn't have stopped it if I tried.

"You made me feel safe for the first time since I had that falling out with Avery. I felt safe from the first moment I saw you, when you saved me from those mutants. And you were annoyed with me, I know. You could barely stand me. But you stayed, and I"—my voice cracked—"I thought it was a sign."

"I'm sorry," he said again. His face was hollow and bleak.

"Did you mean it?"

Confusion flickered over his face. "Mean what?"

"What you said to Nico," I whispered. "That I wasn't a weakness."

Ethan blinked at me, then reached out with a shaking hand to tuck a loose strand of hair behind my ear.

"I meant it," he said lowly, his voice carrying that same deadly edge it had with Nico. "Every word. And I don't care if you *are* something that makes me weak, that takes away my edge. *I don't care.* Because… because…"

He stumbled over his words, and I smiled. "Because I make you happy?"

Ethan laughed under his breath. "Yeah. You do make me happy." His gaze lowered. "And I missed you so much this last week. I'm so sorry for leaving you, Laiken."

I wanted to laugh and cry at the same time. The last week had been a treacherous balance between missing Ethan terribly and cursing him for leaving—it felt nice to have him here, the Vipers a threat no longer.

"Well, if you really mean that, then you'll cut me loose," I said, grinning.

Ethan choked. I grinned again and he whipped out a knife to cut away the bindings. I sighed as I sat up, my wrists bruised and aching. Ethan's gaze never left my face, his eyes pinned on me with such intensity I got the feeling he thought I would drop dead if he looked away.

"I suppose I should say thank you for saving me," I said dryly.

"This shouldn't have happened in the first place," he muttered, kissing my forehead. "I will burn this world to the ground before I let something like this happen to you again."

A surprised laugh escaped me, my fingers twining with his. "I don't doubt you."

It was Ethan's turn to grin, and my heart bloomed to see him happy. But it was gone as quick as it came as his gaze flickered to the body behind me.

Ren. I hadn't saved him, after all. His face was pale, his eyes glassy and unseeing, lying in a pool of his own blood.

"We should get out of here," Ethan said. "I think I got them all, but there might be more hiding out and waiting for the chance to strike."

I nodded. He helped me to my feet, but my vision swirled, and had it not been for Ethan's arms holding me upright, I would have collapsed then and there.

"Are you okay?" he demanded.

"I am far from okay," I said with a wince, "but I'm not seriously injured. Just tired. I haven't slept since they took me." Not well, anyway. My stomach growled. "And I also haven't eaten. Have I mentioned that I am very, very hungry?"

"Did they give you water?"

"Yeah, some. But we might as well add dehydration to the list."

I batted his arms away and used the wall as support to make it to the door. My head swam. I tried to take a step past the double doors, but I stumbled, a fresh wave of nausea gripping me. Ethan wrapped an arm around me before I could fall. He took one look at my face—both of us ignoring the multiple bodies sprawled out around us—and sighed before kneeling down in front of me. "Get on."

I blinked as I realized what he was implying. A smile spread over my lips.

"*Don't,*" he growled.

"You're going to give me a piggyback ride?" I squealed. Oh, he was never going to live this down.

He scowled. "I'd carry you in my arms, but I need them free." He groaned at my expression. "Just hurry up."

My smile only grew wider. I wrapped my arms around his neck, my legs locking around his waist as he stood up with a grunt. I sucked in a breath as I glanced over his shoulder and beheld how far away the ground was.

"I do hope you realize how far off the ground I am," I said. "I mean, this is like being on a stepstool. We are officially in ankle-breaking territory here."

Ethan gave me a dry look. "Duck."

I had exactly half a second to process the meaning of that statement before Ethan ducked through the doorway. The top of the frame nearly clipped my head, and I shrieked, holding onto him for dear life.

"This is actually ridiculous," I informed him.

He handed me the flashlight, his long strides easily carrying us through the halls. "So I've been told."

"Why are short people better than tall people?" I asked.

Ethan remained silent.

"Because they're more down-to-earth."

"Laiken."

"Why is the tallest man in the world so depressed? He has no one to look up to."

"*Laiken.*"

"It's a shame a tall guy like you doesn't have any good tall jokes," I continued. I averted the flashlight beam away from another dead Viper. I decided that I was *not* going to be the person to initiate a conversation about what Ethan had done through the night. I was perfectly content to let that remain his business. "You better get your head out of the clouds and think of some."

"I'm sure there's a Viper still alive somewhere I can hand you over to."

We escaped the building through the front doors and made our way up to the treeline where I assumed Ethan had made camp. Indeed, his big pack dangled from a low-hanging tree branch, a small stockpile of weapons heaped beneath it. I waited until Ethan set me down before springing one last joke on him. "You do know why we had an argument to begin with, right?"

Ethan crossed his arms, humoring me.

I grinned. "It's because we couldn't see *eye-to-eye*."

His eyes narrowed. My smile widened, and a second later, his expression cracked. He turned away, but not before I caught a glimpse of a smile on his face. *Victory.*

Ethan cleaned the blood off his two hunting knives before grabbing his pack and sorting through it. He tossed me a can of soup and ordered me to eat. I did so without another word, my stomach grumbling as he handed me a can opener. He packed light, so there wasn't a ton of food in his stash, but it was enough for my stomach to stop growling at me.

"Wash up," Ethan said, this time giving me two water bottles. "I'm going back to find our stuff."

I almost dropped the water. "Back into the base?"

"Everything from the church is in there, plus whatever supplies they had before. You need new clothes. And since you just ate every bit of food I had left, we're going to need more of that, too."

I winced. "Sorry."

He waved a hand. "Don't be. Just wash up while I'm gone."

"It feels like you're subtly telling me I stink."

Ethan gave me a deadpan look. "You do."

I choked. "Lord a'mercy. Ethan Ellis, your ways with women are phenomenal. However do you manage it?"

He snorted as he sheathed his knives. "Clean up, Laiken. I'll be back in a few minutes."

I watched him walk off through the trees, and a strong sense of déjà vu slammed into me as I remembered him walking off the day we fought. It had been in this exact spot, though that day, he'd taken off in the other direction.

"Be careful," I called after him.

He twisted, walking backwards for a few steps as he called, "I always am."

Then he was gone, vanished between two wide oak trees.

But this time, I comforted myself in the fact that he was coming back.

NINE

He took a lot more than a few minutes, returning with an armful of bags and gear when the sun was in full force. While he was gone, I stripped down and washed off using the bottles of water. But one look at my nasty clothes had me wrinkling my nose in disgust, so I swiped one of Ethan's shirts to wear. It was a worn gray t-shirt with the government insignia on the back—the same shirt he wore on the day we first met, if I remembered correctly. It fell to the middle of my thighs, more than covering everything. But that didn't stop Ethan from tripping over his own feet when he caught sight of me.

"My clothes were dirty," I said by way of explanation. "And I believe someone told me that I stunk."

He chucked one of the bags at my feet. Not just any bag—a familiar blue backpack.

I ripped it open, glad to see everything still in place, including a fresh change of clothes. Ethan turned away as I tugged on a pair of cotton shorts and a new tank top that were soft, but more importantly, *clean.*

"You look better," he noted, piling the gear under a massive oak tree. Most of it I recognized, stuff taken from my church, but he'd dipped into the Viper's stash as well.

I was about to snap back with another reply about his skills with women, but the sight of Ethan's blood-splattered face had me pausing. There was a gash on his head I hadn't noticed in the dark, at least an inch long cut near his hairline that had dripped blood all down the side of his face.

"Hold up," I said, grabbing his arm. "That cut on your head looks awful."

"It's fine," he grunted, stacking up the last of the bags.

"Nope, you don't get to say that. Get down here so I can look at it."

"I'm fine," he said with a roll of his eyes, but then he winced.

I crossed my arms.

Ethan sighed and sat down.

"I'm no expert," I said, probing the wound, "but this looks bad. What happened?"

"I bashed it on the corner of that big table."

I gaped. "How? When?"

"When Nico shot at Ren." He winced again. "I was trying to get to cover. I guess I moved a little too fast, given how dark it was."

I frowned. "Do you think you have a concussion?"

"I'm fine."

"No you're not! I can tell it's hurting you! And it looks *awful*. Try to spell your name out so I can see if your brain is working."

"Laiken—"

I shoved a stick in his hand. "Do it."

Ethan gave me a flat look and scratched *ETHAN ELLIS* into the dirt. "There. I'm perfectly fine. I'm going to grab some more—"

"Oh, no you're not." I shoved him down before he could stand. "You're going to rest, big guy."

"Laiken, I—"

"You look like shit," I said brightly. He did, in fact, look like shit. His clothes were stained with crimson. Blood coated the side of his face from the gash on his head. His blonde hair was mused, one lock standing on end from where he'd run his hands through it, and there was a tiredness in his eyes that needed to go. "Come on, Bull. Get cleaned up so we can rest."

Maybe he was too tired to argue, because he did so without protest. He didn't even scowl at the nickname. He peeled off his blood-stained shirt and tossed it into the fire before tugging on the gray one I'd abandoned. I tidied the camp while he washed the blood and grime off his face. The cut on his head looked much better once the blood was rinsed away, but that didn't stop him from muttering something about a headache before stretching out in the grass and throwing his arm over his eyes.

And he said he was *fine*. I planted my hands on my hips, watching him for a few moments before digging the bottle of whiskey and the glasses out of his pack.

Ethan glanced up as I pressed a glass into his hand, his eyes holding a silent question.

"I figured you could use a pick-me-up," I said.

He held out the glass. "I thought you didn't like this stuff."

"Like you said, it's more about the feeling than the taste." I sat down and poured us each a glass and clinked them to-gether. "Cheers."

The whiskey burned down my throat. I made a face, even while Ethan knocked his back without as much as batting an eye. I put the drink away and laid back. Ethan's eyes were on me. I tucked my arm underneath my head and asked, "So what now?"

He shrugged. "I don't know. I don't really want to go back to the church."

"No, not with what they did to it," I sighed. "My beautiful windows, all destroyed."

Ethan sat up. "Oh, that reminds me."

He dug through his back, producing my wrinkled cowboy hat. I grinned as he placed it on my head.

But I sucked in a breath as he pulled a familiar purple book out and handed it to me.

My sketchbook.

I flipped through the pages. "I didn't remember I left this with you until the next day." A teasing smile played on my lips. "I figured you would have burned it or something because you were mad."

He winced. "I might have thrown it across the room."

I clicked my tongue as I came across a page with a crease in it. "Naughty."

"I looked at it," he added.

"Oh? Was this before or after you chucked it across the room?"

His eyes narrowed, but it quickly faded. "After. I was going to ask you about one of the pictures. It looked like you and your sister, maybe?"

"This one?" I asked, flipping to a portrait in the front of the book. "Yeah, that's my sister, Lucy." I smiled at the picture, recalling the sunny afternoon in which I'd drawn it. The picture showed the two of us sitting on the roof of our house back in Houston, our arms draped over the other's shoulders. My fingers brushed my necklace. "She's the only person I left in Houston that's worth drawing."

Ethan angled his head at the picture, studying it over my shoulder. "You're blonde."

I pinched him. "Naturally blue hair isn't a thing, you know."

"Why blue, though? I mean, why dye your hair at all?"

I lifted a shoulder, running a hand through my still-damp hair. "A few months after I left, I was looking through some department store. Of course, it was ransacked, but a lot of the beauty products were left behind because they're useless when it comes to survival." Ethan looked inclined to agree. I narrowed my eyes at him. "That store had all kinds of different dyes. I saw the blue, the picture of the girl on the front, and I wanted to try it. Because it was so bright and bold and there wasn't anyone around to tell me not to."

I remembered standing in that store, the dust-covered box of dye in my hand, the grinning girl on the label with lucious blue locks. I wanted to be that girl, smiling even while everything was falling apart. Bright and happy, even in the wastelands.

I was a believer in sunny days and starry nights, and I wasn't about to let Avery's memory—and the memory of what he had done—take that from me.

I finished, "I did it once and realized I liked it, so I went back to that store a few weeks later and took their entire inventory of blue hair dye."

Ethan frowned at my hair. "It is certainly bright."

"I wouldn't have done it otherwise."

"It's also a waste of water," he said bluntly. Not rude, just matter-of-fact.

I aimed a kick at him. "I had running water at the church. Stop complaining about decisions I made before I even met you."

Ethan laughed and laid back down. My heart filled to see him smiling. It changed his entire appearance—he looked younger, more handsome, not as stern and callous.

"We could also head back to the ocean," he said, closing his eyes. "It would have been nice the first time, if not for Nico."

"Nico, the storm, your refusal to swim… it was a *great* time, wasn't it?"

He cracked open one eye. "I'll make a deal with you. If we go back to the ocean, I will let you teach me how to swim."

"Really?"

He frowned. "I'm starting to regret this already."

I patted his shoulder. "Oh, you won't regret learning a life-saving skill from the best teacher in the wastelands. We are going to have so much *fun*."

"I'm definitely going to regret this."

"And we are definitely heading straight for the ocean."

"Now?"

"Tomorrow." I shrugged. "Or maybe the next day. That's the amazing thing about not having a schedule—we don't have to be anywhere at any particular time."

"Welcome to the wastelands," Ethan deadpanned.

I smiled and laid down next to him. "You *are* a charmer," I said. His brows flicked up. "Heart of gold. Diamond in the rough. The full package."

"I still don't get what that means," he muttered.

"It means I like you, dumbass," I drawled. I smacked his arm, but Ethan caught my hand and pressed a kiss to my fingers.

"I love you, Laiken," he murmured, his gaze soft for once.

"I love you too, Bull," I said, resting my head in the crook of his shoulder.

His lips curved into a smile. He snaked an arm around me, tugging me close even as his eyes closed. I let the conversation lapse into silence. Ethan had to be tired. I knew I was, and I hadn't spent the entire night killing the Vipers.

I winced at the memory. It already seemed like so long ago, my mind doing well to avoid thinking about it. Ethan might act like it didn't bother him, but I knew it did, deep down. He was still human, after all.

We stayed there for hours. The sun trekked across the sky, eventually dipping below the horizon. We sat up long enough to eat a quick meal—and for Ethan to knock back another shot of the whiskey—before lying right back down again, neither of us in any hurry to do much of anything.

Ethan dozed off by the time the first stars became visible. He was fast asleep when the sky became fully dark, the moon a slash of silver overhead. The sky was black as ink, the stars like a sprinkle of glitter. It was a beautiful, calm night.

The kind of night Lucy and I would go out to watch the stars for hours.

I glanced at Ethan, then back up at the sky, and decided this was even better.

TURN THE PAGE
FOR A
BONUS CHAPTER!

The two Vipers were dead.

They were sprawled on the ground with glassy eyes and unmoving bodies. Ethan towered over them, chest heaving. He was a mess—the front of his t-shirt was drenched in sweat and mutant blood. Icy wrath flickered in his eyes. His hair was mused, his jaw clenched, his hands gripping his weapons tight enough to turn his knuckles white.

It was hard to look at him, so I stared at the atlas in my hands. So many names on it, so many Vipers that were out looking for us. My gaze snagged on Nico's name.

"What do we do now?" I asked, folding up the atlas and tucking it into the back pocket of my denim shorts. "Besides getting you swimming lessons, of course."

If something had forced us into the river flowing only a few feet away, I wasn't kidding myself into thinking I could keep myself *and* all six foot, nine-and-a-half inches of Ethan afloat. But Ethan seemed too distracted to even acknowledge my comment. "This was just a lucky guess. A shot in the dark. Nico doesn't know where we are."

"But what happens when these two don't come back and he sends out a search party for them?" I asked. "They'll find the bodies, the evidence of a fight, and they'll keep searching for us. Nico has a vendetta now. He's going to keep looking until he finds us."

Ethan took the atlas back and studied it. "Not if we find them first."

I choked. "You want to find their base?"

He gave a single curt nod.

"And do what, exactly?" I demanded. "Kill everyone? That seems like a good way to get yourself killed. We don't know how many of them there are or what kind of resources they might have—"

"You underestimate my abilities."

"You're injured," I countered.

He glanced down at the blood seeping from his left arm as if noticing it for the first time. The man took a *bullet* and barely even winced.

"It's not too bad," he said, catching my gaze.

"You are bleeding *everywhere*." I tugged a bandana out of my pocket and pressed it against his arm, wincing at how quickly it soaked through. "Come on, we need to get you patched up before this gets infected."

"I've had worse."

He stepped away, but I grabbed his hand. "Ethan. I am in full support of taking down these no-good Vipers, but we need to recover first, okay?" My jaw clenched. "I mean, you just killed two people. Do you not need a minute to… I don't know, to compose yourself or something?"

Ethan fixed me with a stare so cold that the air temperature plummeted. "I am perfectly composed."

Like hell he was. "We are going back to the church. Now."

His eyes dropped down to my lips for the briefest of seconds before snapping back up. "Okay."

I blinked, having not expected him to fold so quickly. Ethan followed me back through the woods without any further complaint, leaving the two Vipers behind us. I wondered what he planned to do with them, if he would just leave them there, or if he would burn them, or if perhaps he would give them a proper burial.

I decided not to think about that anymore.

The air was heavy with humidity, making it hard to breathe as we walked up the hill to the church. I ordered Ethan to sit on the stage where the pulpit stood while I hunted down a first aid kit. I plopped down in front of him, pulling a roll of gauze from the kit as I frowned at his blood-soaked clothes.

"You're going to need to take off that shirt," I said.

He peeled it off without warning. In the past few weeks, I'd always turned away when I saw Ethan changing, but now I had no excuse to turn away, meaning there was nothing preventing me from getting a full view of his bare torso.

His very muscular torso, might I add. Scars criss-crossed over his chest and abdomen, evidence of dozens of old fights. I ripped my gaze back to his wound as I opened up a fresh water bottle, even as I wondered how he'd gotten those scars, the stories behind those fights.

"It's not bad," Ethan said, oblivious to my failed efforts to stop staring at him. "Just a flesh wound."

That didn't stop me from washing it out thoroughly, trying not to gag at the blood. I wasn't squeamish, but there was a reason I hadn't wanted to follow in Lucy's footsteps and become a nurse. Ethan let out a low hiss as I cleaned off the blood, so I eased my movements, trying to be as gentle as possible.

"I'm no expert," I said, grimacing as I tied off the bandage. "I don't know how to do stitches or anything." Even though that's probably what he needed.

He adjusted the gauze. "It's fine."

I went to stand up, but Ethan's gaze snagged on my cheek. He pulled me back down in a flash. I'd forgotten about the cut on my cheek, but it stung as he lifted a damp cloth to it, gently cleaning it out and treating it with ointment from the first aid kit. He didn't say a word the entire time, his eyes focused on the small injury. His eyes were a nice hazel color, I noted, the light making the green stand out more.

Ethan slowly retracted his hand. "Thanks," I whispered.

"Thanks to you, too," he said, just as quietly.

"We make a pretty good team, don't we, Bull?"

He snorted. "Yeah, I guess we do."

"We should totally do this more often," I added, grinning.

"Beating up bad guys? Heck, yes."

Ethan shook his head. "I don't get it."

"Don't get what?"

"You're always so…" He searched for the word. "*Happy.*"

I arched a brow. "I didn't realize there was anything wrong with that."

He lifted his good arm in a shrug. "We're in the apocalypse. There are mutants roaming everywhere, waiting to kill. Nobody in your hometown understood you, so you decided it was better out here with the monsters than in there. Every day, you slaughter them and pray you survive. And right now, we're stuck battling Nico and his Vipers and worrying they're going to try to slaughter us in our sleep. You just witnessed me kill two of them, and not even fifteen minutes later, you're smiling again. I've spent most of my life miserable, and yet, you're perfectly happy." He sighed. "I just don't get it. I don't get *you.*"

Ethan stared at me with genuine confusion, and I realized he truly meant it.

I ducked my head. "I've always been a half-glass-full kind of person, you know? I've tried the other way; being miserable, being sad, being angry. None of it made me feel good. In a world where things have gone to hell, making yourself feel like hell isn't the answer. So I decided to look on the bright side of things." I smiled at my stained glass windows, lifting one hand and watching a rainbow of colors play across my skin. "And that's what made me feel good inside, so I stuck with it."

Those first couple of weeks after I ran from Houston… I never wanted to relive them. I had spent hours reliving Avery's attack, wondering if there was something I could have done differently, something I could have said to make things better. I'd pondered on it so much I made myself miserable. Avery had ruled over me, even though I was miles away from him. It had been a choice to let it go—to let *him* go, to choose to be happy despite the circumstances. To be happy even in the wastelands. And it was after I made that decision that I realized I didn't want to go back to the Safe Zones.

At least, not yet.

I glanced at Ethan. "And what about you? You just said you've spent most of your life miserable, but you don't seem to make much of an effort to change that. I've known you for a couple of weeks now, and you've only started smiling and laughing in the past few days. Doesn't it feel better to smile? To be happy? To go through life thanking God for everything you have instead of cursing Him for not giving you what you think you want?"

He seemed at a loss for words for a few moments. When he finally did speak, it was a confused, jumbled mess, like he wasn't sure of his own words. "It does feel better. I just—I'm not—" He sucked in a breath. "I don't really know. These past few days with you… It's something I've never experienced before. Something I've never had. I've never met someone quite like you."

I angled my head. "I'm going to assume that's a compliment."

"It is."

I leaned closer to him. "Well, Bull," I drawled, "I've never met anyone quite like you, either. And that's a compliment as well."

Ethan studied my face, his eyes darting back and forth. We were so close, and suddenly I was very aware of him being shirtless in front of me and—

Ethan kissed me.

It was nothing like yesterday's kiss. It had been a gamble to write *Kiss the other contestant* and slip it onto the bottom of the pile. That kiss had been cold and a little unfeeling, leaving Ethan dazed and me disappointed.

But this... It was burning, passionate, all-consuming. I threw my arms around Ethan's neck as he tugged me closer to him, his mouth on mine like I was the air he needed to breathe. His hand shot into my hair. I melted against him, pulling him closer, deepening the kiss until I was out of breath and had to pull back for air. I was smiling harder than I had in a while, dizzy and breathless.

"Happy now?" I asked, still close enough that my lips brushed his.

Ethan's arms tightened around me. "Very."

I pulled back enough to see his face. "The Vipers can wait a little longer, can't they?"

He nodded, just as breathless as I was. "They don't know anything is amiss for a few days." He slid a hand down my back. "You're right, by the way."

"About what?"

"In a world that's gone to hell, making yourself feel like hell isn't the answer."

Hearing my own words echoed back to me by him was enough to bring a smile to my face. I traced a finger down his jaw, soaking in every detail. "I am usually right about those kinds of things. I am the queen of happiness."

He rolled his eyes at my exaggerated wink. "I don't think anyone is competing with you for that title."

My grin widened. Ethan's expression softened, just a touch, and that was all I needed to tug him closer. He angled his mouth over mine, and I found myself wishing that we could trap ourselves in this moment, in this kiss. No more mutants, no more wastelands, no more Vipers, no more thoughts about ex-boyfriends that tried to kill me. I wanted to do this forever.

Ethan kissed me again, and it felt like the world was falling apart around us, shattering into a million fragments that fell away, leaving nothing but the two of us in a church with homemade stained glass windows. It wasn't much. It wasn't perfect.

But it was all I needed.

ABOUT THE AUTHOR

JAYDEN THOMPSON first discovered her love of writing at fifteen years old. Her first novel, *Diamond in the Rough*, was published when she was eighteen. A Kentucky native, Jayden spends her time reading, hanging out with family, watching too many YouTube videos, and daydreaming about fictional worlds.

For sneak peeks of upcoming books and more content, you can check out her YouTube channel (@jaydenthompsonauthor), her Instagram (@authorjaydenthompson), and her website (jaydenthompson.com).

SZOA